D1123102

Big Brother Now

For two heroes: my beloved husband, Harry; and my own dear big brother, David — AS

For Sofia — KM

Published by
MAGINATION PRESS
An Educational Publishing Foundation Book
American Psychological Association
750 First Street, NE
Washington, DC 20002

For more information about our books, including a complete catalog, please write to us, call 1-800-374-2721, or visit our website at www.maginationpress.com.

Editor: Becky Shaw
Art Director: Susan K. White
Printed by Phoenix Color, Rockaway, New Jersey

Library of Congress Cataloging-in-Publication Data

Sheldon, Annette.
Big brother now : a story about me and our new baby / by Annette Sheldon ; illustrated by Karen Maizel.
p. cm.
ISBN-13: 978-1-4338-0381-9 (hardcover : alk. paper)
ISBN-10: 1-4338-0381-X (hardcover : alk. paper)
ISBN-13: 978-1-4338-0382-6 (pbk. : alk. paper)
ISBN-10: 1-4338-0382-8 (pbk. : alk. paper) 1. Infants–Juvenile literature. 2. Brothers and sisters–Juvenile literature. 3. Parent and child–Juvenile literature. I. Maizel, Karen. II. Title.

HQ774.S538 2008
306.875–dc22   2008017554

10 9 8 7 6 5 4 3 2 1

Big Brother Now

A Story About Me and Our New Baby

written by Annette Sheldon
Illustrated by Karen Maizel

MAGINATION PRESS • WASHINGTON, D.C.
American Psychological Association

"You're such a wonderful boy!"
Everybody used to tell me that.
I liked hearing them say it.
It made me feel warm
and safe and strong.

Now I have a baby sister.
Her name is Abby.
Now everybody talks
goo-goo and brings
Abby presents. Well,
sometimes for me, too.
The whole house is full
of pink stuff.
Now, everybody tells
me, "Jake, you're a
wonderful big brother!"
I don't know how to be
a big brother.

My granddad lives next door. I call him Pop-Pop.
He used to call me up every day, after he closed his
bicycle shop, and say, "How's my Champ?" Now, on his
way home from the bicycle shop, he stops in and asks
right away, "How is my baby Abby doing?
And where's my Champ?"

Nothing works around here like it used to. I ask Mom to help me make my snack. She says, "Pretty soon, Jake. I need to finish feeding Abby. She is so little; she doesn't know how to wait yet." So I wait.

I wash the apple.

Mom's still busy.

I get out the apple cutter.

We need a paper towel, too.

When Abby finishes, Mom uses the apple cutter. She tells me, "You're a good big brother to wait patiently, Jake. I know sometimes it's hard. It was a good idea to get things ready while you waited." I like it when Mom says that.

One day the wind is too cold to go outside.

Before, Mom and I would read on those cold days.

But Abby is fussy again.
She cries really hard.
I wait while Mom
walks with her.
Mom is telling her,
"Whshshsh-whsh.
Whshshsh-whsh."

I ask Mom why she does that. She says it sounds like her heartbeat Abby heard before she was born. It's supposed to make her feel better.

It's not working.

Mom walks and walks. Abby cries a long time.
She turns red and gets the hiccups.
Finally, I walk, too.

I try humming for her.

Then Mom even helps me hum,
but I think Abby can't hear us.

Finally, my little sister feels better and falls asleep. After Mom tucks Abby into her crib, she flops down and says, "Jake, I'm sorry. I'm just too tired to read. Climb up here and keep me company while I rest for a few minutes. Then we'll read your book."

While Mom rests,
I look at the
firefighter heroes
in my book.

Then I run my trucks
with the sirens off.

On Fridays, Mom takes me to my story time at the library. Abby comes with us, but she is not old enough to come in for the story.

On Saturdays Dad and I take care of Abby, so Mom can go to lunch with Aunt Sue and Gran. When Abby gets hungry, she wants to eat right away, so we hurry to get her bottle.

If her special milk spills, I wipe it up for Dad. Our cat, Momo, likes to help with that. Dad gets more milk from the fridge and says, "Jake, thanks for the help. You are getting really good at this big brother stuff."

When I hear Abby fussing, I reach through into her crib and pat her.
I tell her, "Whshshsh-whsh. Whshshsh-whsh. I'm right here. You're okay."
She opens her eyes and looks at me for a long time. Then she smiles a
little, and falls asleep again. It worked! I do feel like a big brother now!

When I leave her room, Dad is in the doorway.

He gives me a high five,

and we do our secret wild man dance.

25

Pop-Pop calls this morning.
He asks how Abby is, but this
time he wants to talk to me, too.
He wants someone to go with
him to the bike shop to help out
a little. He says while we're
there, we're going to shine up
my bike, and put a horn on it!

Abby isn't ready for anything fun like going with Pop-Pop because she is just a baby.

But I'm ready for it.
So I'll go with
Pop-Pop to the
bike shop.

And I feel warm and safe and strong.

Note to Parents

by JANE ANNUNZIATA, PSY.D.

A new baby in the family is a source of joy for everyone. Older brother and sisters usually welcome the arrival with their own brand of excitement, wonder, pride, caring, and affection, just as their parents do. At the same time, however, their world is changing in ways they don't understand and can't control, and along with such changes comes an array of less happy feelings, including anger, jealousy, resentment, confusion, and fear that Mom and Dad don't love them as much now.

Older children may express these negative feelings by regressing—by behaving like a baby (or a much younger child), and wanting to be treated like one. They may also act out their anger by throwing tantrums, pinching the baby, or breaking the baby's toys or their parents' things. Or they may do just the opposite and try to be the perfect child or perfect big sister or brother, trying to regain the spot they fear they've lost in their parents' hearts. These feelings and reactions can be intense—and they are entirely normal, if not inevitable. In addition to keeping a sense of humor, here are a few things that parents can do to help ease the transition.

Before the Baby Arrives

Prepare your older child about the baby before the arrival, and start earlier rather than later. Advance work goes a long way toward helping the older child's adjustment.

If you know the sex of the new baby, it is helpful to let your child know this ahead of time. A new baby of the same sex can bring up positive feelings when the child views the sibling as a future friend who will have similar interests, or it can increase the jealousy and resentment for some children because it makes them feel less "special." Conversely, a new baby of the opposite sex preserves the uniqueness of the child's role, but can lead to worries that a baby of the opposite sex is more "special" and "desired/desirable" and thus will be more cherished. Addressing these worries and fantasies, and providing reassurance will go a long way toward resolving any concerns.

Visit the hospital with your child, and take advantage of any sibling classes your hospital or doctor may offer to demystify the event and soothe your child's anxiety.

Explain what a baby can and cannot do so that fantasies aren't disappointed. An ideal way to do this is to cuddle up together and read books or pamphlets about babies, reminiscing, telling stories about, and looking at photographs and other mementos of the older child while you read.

Let your child know who will be caring for him or her, how long Mom will be gone, when Dad will be home, when the child can visit Mom and see the baby, and any other questions he or she may have.

Concrete, visual reminders are especially comforting. Write out the plan and post it. Even children who are too young to read are reassured by its existence and can ask to have it read and reread to them. This will help the child feel as cherished as the new baby.

After the Baby Is Home

Set aside one-on-one time with your older child as much as possible. Even if it's just 15 minutes a day or one afternoon a week, exclusive time with Mom and Dad, separately and together, is important. Tell your child how glad you are to have this special time together.

Gently and at appropriate moments, remind your child of the benefits of being "bigger." You can say, "Babies only get to drink milk. They can't eat

30

ice cream like you do," or "Your sister is too little to go swimming with us. She won't be able to go until she is bigger like you." This can help when the child is feeling jealous or wants to be a baby.

Involve the help and support of extended family (e.g. grandparents) and friends, to provide extra fun time and nurturance for your child.

Include your child in some decisions, both before and after the arrival. When children have some say ("Should we buy a yellow blanket or a striped one?"), they feel more involved. This can help with feelings of lack of control. Be careful not to overdo, though. This can lead to resentment about all the special purchases and time being spent on the baby.

Keep the same rules, rituals, and schedules that you had before, so that the world stays as predictable and stable as possible. Expect to have rules challenged more than usual, however.

Try not to change the older child's

room, which can cause feelings of displacement. If you must move the child, do it months before the arrival. And if the child is moved or has to share a room with the baby, give him or her as much control as possible with furnishing and so forth. Even a simple line of masking tape or a curtain hanging in the middle of the room can help preserve a sense that "at least part of this is still mine."

Developmental challenges such as potty training or riding a bike without training wheels usually go more smoothly (and more successfully!) if they're not attempted after the birth of a sibling. Your child is already under stress from the addition of a new baby to the family and won't respond well to yet another challenge. Your child will feel better about and respond best to one life change at a time!

Ask your child for help from time to time—bring a diaper or sing a song to the baby. If the child wants to push the stroller or hold the baby, facilitate doing so safely and make sure the rules are clear. This fosters the child's feelings of importance and helps establish sibling bonds.

Avoid giving your child too much responsibility, which can cause resentment. On the other hand, if the child seeks excessive responsibility, trying to

win your love, give lots of reassurance that you love him or her just the way he or she is. Tell the child that being the parent is your job, not the child's, even though he or she may be a big sister or brother now.

Offer fun alternatives when the child can't do something because of the baby. For example, if the baby is sleeping and the child must be quiet, offer to bake cookies or read a book together.

Address as much as possible your child's valid complaints about the baby. If the baby wakes the child at night, for example, look for solutions such as shutting the door or running a noise screen. Not only does the problem get solved, but the child also learns that the parents are devoted to meeting his or her needs as well as the baby's.

When the going gets rough, as it often does, it may help to remember that your child is behaving in ways that are to be expected. It can even be calming to the child to be told directly, "It's okay to feel mad at your brother sometimes. All children feel that way when they're getting used to a new brother or sister."

JANE ANNUNZIATA, Psy.D., is a clinical psychologist with a private practice for children and families in McLean, Virginia. She is also an author of several books addressing the special needs of children and parents.

31

About the Author

Happily retired after 19 years in public libraries as a storyteller and preschool specialist, Annette Sheldon lives and writes on a farm in Austinburg, Ohio, with her husband, Harry.

About the Illustrator

Karen Maizel has illustrated 21 books for children and teaches foundational courses at an art and design college. She lives with her husband near Cleveland, Ohio, and has three grown daughters and a granddaughter.